Enid Blyton's
Five-Minute
Bedtime Tales

Illustrated by Roger De Klerk

Award Publications Limited

For further information on Enid Blyton please visit
www.blyton.com

ISBN 978-1-84135-532-0

This edition entitled **Enid Blyton's Five-Minute Bedtime Tales**
published by permission of Chorion Rights Limited

This edition first published 2008

Published by Award Publications Limited,
The Old Riding School, The Welbeck Estate,
Worksop, Nottinghamshire, S80 3LR

www.awardpublications.co.uk

10 2

Printed in China

Contents

Corovell, the Children's Dust-Man

Once upon a time, long, long ago, the world became so full of exciting happenings that the children could not go to sleep at night. Mothers and fathers began to get worried. The fairies too were anxious, for when the children did not sleep they became cross and tired and, of course, could not see any fairies. And the fairies did not like that at all, for they loved playing with the children.

So the King of the Fairies called a great meeting, to which all the fairies, big and little, came. "I will offer a reward," said the king, "to any fairy who can find something to make all the children go to sleep at the proper time."

All the fairies were very excited. They began to make plans at once.

"I know what I shall do," said one. "I shall string some baby stars together, and hold them in front of the children's eyes. They will be so dazzled with starshine that they will fall asleep at once."

"I don't think much of that idea," said another fairy. "I'm going to find the magic words in an old book and make them into a sleep-song. Then I shall sing it, and all the children will go to sleep listening to me."

Each fairy had a different idea, and each began to try to do what he or she had planned. The necklace of baby stars was no use, for the brightness made the children more awake than ever. The magic sleep-song did send some of them to sleep, but it kept others awake.

Another fairy tried stroking the children's hair very softly; but while it brought sleep to some, it fidgeted others. Other fairies danced softly round the candles in the children's bedrooms, but they were so interested in watching the fairies that they became more wide awake than ever.

The fairies began to feel that there was really nothing to be done, and one by one they gave up trying. Great gloom settled over Fairyland, for the tired children were much too cross ever to play with the fairies in the daytime.

Now all this time there was one little fairy called Corovell who was very busy indeed. All one day he was scraping the bloom off the darkest red roses he could find in Fairyland, and shaking it down into a yellow sack he was carrying. On another day he went to all the blue butterflies he knew, and begged them each to give him a little powder from one of their wings. Because they liked little Corovell they shook some of their powder into his outstretched hands, and flew off into the sunshine. Corovell carefully mixed it with the rose bloom in his sack.

The next morning he scraped the sunshine from the top of all the little puddles shining in the sun. This he mixed carefully with some black powder from the middle of bright red poppies.

He took the softest and brightest green moss growing on the palace wall and powdered it into tiny, tiny pieces. Then he mixed into it the magic scent of the June wild roses, and shook it all up together with the other powders and dust. As he was carrying the sack along through the wood that night he picked out a star shining in a puddle and put it into his sack, just for luck. To finish off, he stirred it all up well with the brightest feather from a kingfisher's breast.

When Corovell was satisfied with his mixture, he took his yellow sack on his shoulders and went to the king's palace.

"Your Majesty," he said, bowing low, "I have discovered something which will make any child sleepy."

"Prove it," said the king eagerly.

Corovell flew to a nursery full of naughty, tired children.

"Now watch," he said softly. He dipped his hand into his sack, and pulling out a handful of glittering dust, he sprinkled some of it into each child's eyes.

The baby child fell asleep at once. The next smallest crept over to her mother and, laying her head down, went to sleep. All the other children stopped quarrelling and began to rub their eyes, saying, "Oh, I am so sleepy."

"Well done!" said the king. "It is a wonderful discovery. What is your sleep-dust made of?"

Corovell told him. "And," he said, "it not only makes the children go to sleep, but it makes them dream of roses and butterflies and poppies and starshine – all the beautiful things in the world."

"Splendid!" cried the king. "The children will soon be happy in the daytime now, so we can play with them again. What will you have for your reward?"

"Make me the children's dust-man," said the little fairy, kneeling down before the king. "Grant that I may be their special night-time friend, and that they may all know and love me."

"Very well, that shall be your reward," answered the king. "You shall be the children's dust-man and make the children sleepy at night-time, so that the next day they will not be too tired to see us when we come to play with them."

And every night since then, as quick as the gleam on a dragonfly's wing, along comes Corovell the dust-man with his yellow sack of magic sleep-dust. He sprinkles some of it into every child's eyes and they grow sleepier and sleepier, and at last fall softly asleep to dream of flowers and birds, butterflies and starshine, until daytime peeps in through the window.

The Tale of the Goldfish

Once upon a time, thousands of years ago, there lived in China a merchant who was very fond of fishes. He kept four big ponds and in each swam a different kind of fish, some little, some big, some brightly-coloured and some speckled with silver spots. The merchant loved his fish and fed them every day.

He liked his brightly-coloured fish the best. There were some that had blue streaks down their sides and others that seemed to have caught a rainbow in their tails. The merchant leaned over his ponds to watch his fish and longed for one thing – to breed a fish that was bright gold from nose to tail!

"There are plenty of silver fish!" he said to himself. "There are many rainbow-coloured fish, and others that are spotted and speckled with brilliance. But no one in the whole world has ever had a fish that was all gold. How lovely it would be! How everyone would marvel! There could never be a prettier fish than a gold one, and it would give pleasure to people everywhere."

So he tried very hard to rear a fish that was all gold. But he found it was impossible. Some fish had bright yellow spots on them, some had orange-coloured streaks, but none was all gold from tip to tail.

The merchant fell on bad times. He lost a great deal of his money and became poor and shabby. He shut up his large house and lived in a small corner of it, without servants to wait on him.

But he did not forget to feed his fish. He became an old man and gave up the idea of rearing a fish of gold. He found that he was happy even though he was poor, and when his little grandchildren came to see him and climbed on his knees to listen to his stories, he wished for nothing better.

One night a strange traveller came to the old merchant's house. The great bell outside the gate jangled to and fro as it had not done for years, and the merchant heard it in surprise. Who could be coming to his house now? He had no rich friends; they had all forsaken him.

He went through the long passages that led to the front gate and unbarred it. Outside stood a cloaked man, his horse beside him.

"Does Wong Fu, the great merchant, live here?" asked the visitor in a deep voice.

"Honourable sir, it is Wong Fu you see before you," said the merchant, bowing, "but I am no longer great. I am a poor man and my house is empty. Enter, I pray you, for I will find you shelter and food, though it will not be of grand quality."

The visitor stepped inside. The merchant took him to a great marble basin where he might wash, and then slipped out to see to the horse. He stabled it in the empty stable, gave it food to eat and then went to prepare a meal for his unexpected guest. In an old chest he had a few dainties stored away and these he took out. Soon he had a meal ready and went to call his visitor.

He found him leaning over the ponds, looking at the fish in the moonlight.

"You are fond of your fish, I see," said the visitor, raising his head. "They come swimming up to my hand, tame and friendly."

"Yes," said the merchant. "It has always been the dream of my life to breed a fish all gold from head to tail – but I have never done so. Come, honourable sir, your supper is prepared."

They sat down to eat, and at last the visitor told the old merchant who he was and why he had come.

"I am Sing Fu," he said, "the son of the old washerwoman you had many years ago."

"But you are a wealthy man, well-favoured and wise," said the old merchant in astonishment.

"It is so," said the visitor. "My mother put me in the service of Lai Tu, the famous magician, and I found favour in his sight so that he made me as a son to him. Now Lai Tu is dead, and I have his wealth and much of his learning."

The merchant got up and bowed himself to the ground, until his forehead touched the floor. He was in great awe of enchanters and he trembled to think that he had one in his shabby house.

"Rise," said the visitor. "Do not kneel to me. My mother would not have you do that."

"And is your honourable mother still alive and well?" asked the merchant, seating himself again but still trembling in his surprise and excitement.

"She is well and happy," the enchanter said gravely. "It is by her request that I have come to see you. Do you remember her, honourable host?"

"Yes," said the merchant at once. "She was fat and jolly. She washed my linen better than anyone else."

"And do you remember when she fell ill and could not work for five weeks?" asked the visitor.

The merchant felt uncomfortable. Had he treated the old washerwoman kindly? He could not remember. It would be dreadful if she had sent her son to punish him for an unkindness done to her years ago.

"No, I do not remember that," he said at last.

"My mother remembers," said the magician. "You picked her up and carried her up to bed. You sent a doctor to make her well again, and you paid her wages all the weeks that she could not work. She has never forgotten. And now that she has a son who is wealthy and powerful she has asked me to go to all those who were kind to her and reward them. So I have come to you."

The old merchant was amazed.

"And do you also visit those who treated your mother ill?" he asked. "Do you punish as well as reward?"

"No, for such is not my mother's wish," the enchanter replied gravely. "She has forgotten her enemies but not her well-doers. Now, honourable friend, you are poor and shabby. I bring you riches and honour and they will bring you happiness."

"There you are wrong," said the merchant quietly. "Neither riches nor honour bring happiness. I am happy now, without them. I do not want gold, nor do I want servants, rich food, embroidered clothes. I am old and tired, but I am happy. Leave me as I am."

The magician looked at the old man in wonder. Never before had he met anyone who refused what he had to offer. He said nothing more and, bidding the merchant goodnight, lay down on a mat to sleep.

But in the middle of the night he went to his horse and took a sack from its back. In this sack were great bars of gold which he had brought as a present for the old man. Now they would not be wanted. But the magician had thought of something splendid to do with them.

He took them to one of the ponds, where pretty grey-green fish were swimming, and one by one he slid the bars of gold into the water, murmuring magic words as he did so. Each bar dissolved into a cloud of orange-gold, and behold, the fishes were attracted by the strange mist in the water and swam up in shoals to see what it was.

And when morning came, each fish was bright orange-gold from head to tail! The old merchant saw them when searching for his midnight visitor, who had strangely disappeared. He stood by the pond, amazed and delighted. His dream had come true at last! Here were goldfish – bright gold from nose to tail!

And when you see a gleaming goldfish, remember the kind-hearted merchant and his old washerwoman, and be kind to others yourself. You never know what magic you may start!

The Blackbirds' Secret

Did you know that the blackbird family have a secret that they never tell any other bird or any other creature?

Hundreds of years ago, the Prince of White Magic wanted to mend his Well of Gold. This was a strange and curious well which, so long as history tells, had always been full of pure golden water. Anything that was dipped into this water became as bright and shining as gold and was beautiful to see. But, because of so many, many years of usage, the well water had become poor and no longer seemed to have the golden power it once used to have.

So the prince decided to go to the Land of Sunlight and buy enough pure golden rays to make his well golden again. He set off, taking with him a special thick sack so that the sunlight would not be able to shine through the sack and so give away his secret. He bought what he wanted, and by his enchantment

imprisoned the sunny gold in the sack. He tied it up tightly and set off home again.

But somehow his secret journey to the Land of Sunlight became known and the Yellow-Eyed Goblins, who lived in the Dark Forest, decided to waylay the prince as he passed through their kingdom and rob him of the sack. Then they would use it for the Dark Forest, and make it light and beautiful.

Now the prince had made himself invisible but he could not make the sack unseen. Also, much to his dismay, he found that it was not thick enough, after all, to stop the golden rays from shining through. He would very easily be seen in the Dark Forest. What was he to do?

He called a blackbird to him and asked his advice, and the bird thought of a splendid idea at once. He would ask each blackbird in the forest to spare a black feather from his wing and, with the sticky glue that covered the chestnut buds on the trees, they would stick the dark feathers all over the sack and so hide the brightness inside.

In a second this was done. With the help of the blackbirds and the chestnut glue the prince soon covered the sack with their black feathers, and it was impossible to see it in the darkness of the gloomy forest.

Thus he passed safely through the kingdom of the Yellow-Eyed Goblins, for not one of those crafty little creatures caught a glimpse of either the prince or his black-feathered sack.

The sunlight gold was emptied into the old well and at once the water gleamed brightly. Anything dipped into it became a shining orange-gold, beautiful to see. The prince was delighted. He called the kind blackbirds to him and spoke to them.

"You have helped me," he said, "and now I will reward you. All birds like to be beautiful in the springtime and wear bright feathers – but you are black and cannot beautify yourselves. Still, you may make your big beaks lovely to see – so when the springtime comes near, blackbirds, fly to this well and dip your beaks into the golden water. Then you will have bright, shining beaks of orange-gold."

And every year since then the blackbirds have flown in springtime to the secret golden well, and have come back to us with shining golden beaks.

A Pair of Blue Trousers

Have you ever heard people say, "It will be fine weather today if we can see enough blue sky to make a sailor a pair of trousers"? We often say that, and we look anxiously upwards to see if there is just a little blue patch showing. I wonder if you know how the saying first began?

One year, long ago, there came a terrible spell of cold, cloudy weather. Not a patch of blue sky was to be seen. The weather-clerk was in a very bad temper and he wouldn't send even a speck of blue anywhere. People were in despair and couldn't think what to do.

At last they went to an old wise woman who lived in her tumbledown cottage on the very top of Breezy Hill.

"Can you tell us what to do?" they asked. "We do so badly want good weather."

The old wise woman sat down in her chimney-corner and thought for a while. Then she said, "If you can make the weather-clerk put a patch of blue in the sky big enough to make a sailor a pair of trousers, the weather will turn fine again. That is all I can tell you."

Everyone puzzled over this, and no one could think how to make the weather-clerk put a little patch of blue into the heavens. But at last a sailor-boy stood up and grinned.

"I'll manage it for you," he said. "I've heard that the weather-clerk keeps a snappy dog outside his house. I'll pay the clerk a visit and see if his dog will snap a hole in my trousers. Then I'll go in and demand a new pair, and see what I can get out of him."

So off he went – and you should have heard him growl at the snappy dog, who, of course, growled back and flew at the sailor's trousers. It wasn't long before there was a big hole in them.

The sailor-boy marched up to the front door and crashed the knocker down several times. The door flew open and the weather-clerk looked out angrily. But before he could speak, the sailor began to shout at the top of his voice:

"Look here, look here! See the hole your dog has made in my trousers. You should have that dog locked up, he is a dangerous animal. You must pay me five pieces of gold for my trousers so that I may get a new pair."

"Nonsense," said the clerk, and made as if he would shut the door. But the sailor put his foot in so that he couldn't, and began to shout again, so that the clerk was absolutely terrified.

"Be quiet, pray be quiet," he begged. "You are noisier than a thunderstorm. I have no money to give you for a new pair of trousers."

"Well, I must have a pair!" roared the sailor. "Give me a bit of blue sky to make myself a new pair. Then I will not charge you anything. Quickly, now, before I fetch the policeman to your dog!"

The weather-clerk, shivering and shaking, pulled two clouds apart, and a bit of blue sky peeped between them. The sailor thanked him and ran off in glee. "Look at the blue sky, look at it!" everyone cried in delight. "The first we have seen for months!"

"Yes, I got it for you," said the sailor-boy. "I won't use it for my trousers because you need it for good weather. But please buy me a new pair!"

So they did; and now, on a cloudy day, look up into the sky and see if you can spy a bit of blue big enough to make a sailor a pair of trousers. If you can, you'll see good weather before long.

What! No Cheese?

There was once a little bird who loved cheese. He thought it was far, far nicer than butter, and if he could steal some, he would!

He flew into the grocer's shop and pecked a big hole in the cheese there.

He sat on Dame Tippy's shopping basket as she went home and pecked a big piece out of her bit of cheese, too.

And do you know, he even went into Old Man Dingle's garden and pecked the tiny bits of cheese out of the mouse-traps set there to catch mice who ate the peas! Wasn't he a thief?

He ate so much cheese that he grew quite yellow, and people began to call him the cheese-bird.

They thought he was a greedy little thing, and if ever he came to tea with them they made sure not to have any cheese, for if they did he would eat up every scrap.

So when he popped into their houses and they offered him
bread and butter, or bread and jam, he would put his head on
one side, look down his beak in a very haughty manner, and say,
"What! No cheese?"

He went to tea with Dame Frilly, and she gave him egg
sandwiches. "What! No cheese?" he cried, and wouldn't eat a
thing.

He went to supper with Dickory-Dock, who had a nice meal
of sardines and cocoa ready.

"What! No cheese?" cried the greedy bird, and he wouldn't
touch anything at all.

It seemed such a waste of a meal, because Dickory-Dock
couldn't possibly eat it all himself.

One day the pixie Long-Legs gave a fine party. There were strawberries and cream, vanilla ices and lemonade, and you would have thought anyone would have been pleased, wouldn't you?

But the little yellow bird turned up his beak at everything. "What! No cheese?" he cried again.

Long-Legs was angry. "No," she said, "there isn't any cheese, you greedy little bird. Who stole cheese from the grocer? Who stole Old Man Dingle's mouse-trap cheese? Go away, you greedy thing, and don't come back here again! Sing a song about cheese if you want to – *we* shan't listen."

So the little bird had to fly away into our world. There he found that people were as kind as could be and put out crumbs and potato and coconut and fat – but, of course, not a scrap of cheese!

And so all day long he sits on the telegraph wires, or on a high hedge, and sings the same little song over and over again. "Little bit of bread and no cheese! Little bit of bread and no cheese! Little bit of bread and no cheese!"

Have you heard him? He is singing it this summer just as usual, for I've heard him three times already today.

We call him the yellowhammer and he is a bird rather like a sparrow, but yellow . . . and how he sings the little song:

"Little bit of bread and no cheese!" Do see if you can hear him. He sings it as plainly as anything.

The Pixies and the Primroses

Once upon a time the King of the Fairies complained that primroses were too pale a yellow.

"They are such pretty flowers," he said. "It is a shame to make them look so pale and washed-out. I would like them to be as yellow as the daffodils. The daffodils are beautiful with their deep yellow trumpets."

"Your Majesty," said Scatterbrain the pixie, bowing low. "Will you let me have the job of painting all the primroses a lovely deep yellow? My friends and I can do this easily. I have a special sunshine paint that will be just the colour."

"I don't know if I can trust you to do a job like that," said the king doubtfully, looking at the little pixie. "You know how forgetful you are, Scatterbrain. Why, only this morning you forgot to put any sugar on my porridge, and when I told you about it you shook the salt-cellar over the plate! If I let you do this job you would probably paint the primroses sky-blue or something silly like that."

"Your Majesty, you hurt me very much when you talk like that," said Scatterbrain, going very red. "All I have to do is to give out the paint to my friends, and by the morning the job will be done. Every primrose in the woods will be finished! You will be delighted."

"Very well," said the king. "You may do the work, Scatterbrain – but do be careful!"

Scatterbrain was overjoyed. He called all his pixie friends and told them of the work the king had given them. "Come to me tonight and I will give you each a pot of yellow paint," said the little pixie.

So that night all the pixies went to Scatterbrain's house. He

had been mixing his yellow paint that day and had a big pot of it. He poured some into hundreds of small pots and gave one to each pixie, with a nice new brush. Off they all ran to the woods.

"I haven't done anything silly this time," thought Scatterbrain as he emptied the last lot of paint into a tiny pot for himself. "Won't the king be pleased in the morning when he sees the primroses as yellow as daffodils!"

The pixies set to work. They began in the middle of each primrose and painted very carefully. The deep yellow colour looked lovely.

They went on painting; and then they began to look rather alarmed. Their paint pots were very tiny and only held a little paint. By the time they had painted all round the centre of the primroses there was no more paint left in anyone's pot.

And so, by the time the morning came and the king went to walk in the wood to see what sort of job Scatterbrain had made of the primroses, he found that each of them had a pretty, deep yellow centre – but that was all!

"Your Majesty, I didn't give the pixies enough paint," said Scatterbrain, ashamed. "Let me make some more and finish the primroses."

"Certainly not," said the king. "You would only make another muddle of some kind! The primroses are quite pretty with a deep yellow bit in the middle. Leave them as they are."

So they were left. You can still see the little bit of deep yellow paint in the centre of each one.

Ripple gets a Necklace

Ripple was a water-pixie. She lived in the Long Pond where the waterlilies grew, and she was as pretty as a picture and as proud as a peacock. She swam in the pond all day long, talked to the big frogs, tickled the old fish, and teased the moorhens that came to nest there.

"You know, Ripple would be so nice if she wasn't so conceited," said the water vole one day, as he sat nibbling a water plant. "She's always showing off."

"She cuts the waterlily leaves to pieces, trying to make herself new dresses every week," said the moorhen, pecking a bit of the vole's plant. "Do you think it is safe to nest here this spring, water vole? Last year Ripple kept tipping my babies out of their nest whenever I swam off. It didn't really matter because they could swim as soon as they were hatched – but it made them so tired having to climb back a score of times a day."

"Oh, Ripple doesn't care how she teases anyone," said the vole. "She tied a water beetle and a dragonfly grub together the other day, and they were so angry that they nearly ate each other! She's so vain that she thinks she can do anything."

Now the next day Bufo, the large old toad who lived under a big stone on the bank of the pond, invited everyone in the pond to a party at his end. They were to come and have games and fun. Ripple was invited, too, and she at once began to think what kind of dress she could make for herself.

"I shall be the prettiest person there," she said. "All the others are ugly. I'll have a new dress, and a new ribbon in my hair, and a new necklace."

Well, she cut up five lily leaves for a dress. The lilies were angry for the leaves were new and a very pretty red colour underneath. But Ripple didn't care!

She asked the waterweed for a ribbon and tied it in her waving hair. Now for a necklace. "I'll get some water-snail shells and thread them together," she said.

"Oh no, you won't!" said the snails, and they went to hide.

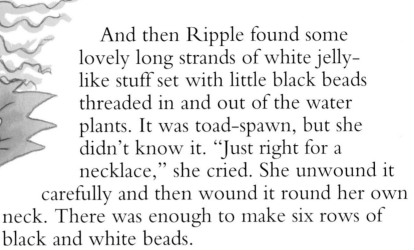

And then Ripple found some lovely long strands of white jelly-like stuff set with little black beads threaded in and out of the water plants. It was toad-spawn, but she didn't know it. "Just right for a necklace," she cried. She unwound it carefully and then wound it round her own neck. There was enough to make six rows of black and white beads.

Ripple was delighted and very proud. She couldn't think why everyone laughed when they saw her! The party day was the next day, very bright and warm and sunny. Ripple went along with everyone else to old Bufo, the toad. He frowned when he saw her and seemed very cross. But Ripple didn't care. She knew she looked beautiful in her new dress and necklace.

And then she felt something tickling her. Something wriggled down her front and something wriggled down her back! She screamed.

"What is it? There's something crawling all over me."

And indeed there was – for the toad-spawn necklace had hatched into tadpoles that had wriggled down her neck! There were dozens of them, little black things that tickled all the time.

"It serves you right," said Bufo, looking as black as thunder. "How dare you come to my party wearing a necklace of toad's eggs? Go home at once!"

Ripple didn't go home. She ran right away from that pond, for she was so ashamed of herself. So the moorhen has built her nest there once again, for now she knows that her nestlings will be safe!

Spot and the Biscuit Tin

Spot was a little brown and white dog. He belonged to Timothy and Judy, and he loved his little master and mistress very much. He sat up with his two ears cocked to listen to what they were saying.

"It's Baby's birthday tomorrow," Judy said. "I'd forgotten all about it. What shall we buy her, Timmy?"

"Let's look in our money-box and see how much we've got," said Timmy. So they took down the pig that held their pennies and unscrewed its head. Out fell two pennies and two two-pence pieces.

"Ooh, only sixpence!" said Timmy, in surprise. "How's that, Judy?"

"Oh, don't you remember, we took some out last week to buy flowers for that old lady who was ill," said Judy. "Oh dear! Sixpence won't buy Baby very much, will it? And I did so want to get her one of those soft, cuddly bunnies in the toyshop. I know she would love that."

Just then their mother came into the room and looked at the children with a smile.

"Counting your money?" she said. "Well, how much have you got for Baby's birthday?"

"Only sixpence!" Judy said sadly. "I do wish it was lots more, Mummy. How can we get any more?"

"You'd better try and find old Mr Giles's silver spoons and forks," said Mummy, with a laugh. "They were stolen from his house last night, and the burglars must have packed them in a biscuit tin for they had emptied the biscuits on the table and the tin was gone. The burglars were caught, but they had buried the tin somewhere and won't say where. Whoever can find it will get a reward."

"Oh, wouldn't it be lovely if we could find it!" said Judy in excitement. "But I'm sure we can't."

Spot, the little dog, was listening hard to everything that was said. As soon as he heard about the biscuit tin, he wagged his tail. He knew what a biscuit tin was, and he knew the smell of it, too. He would try to find it for them!

He licked Judy's hand and tugged at her skirt.

"I do believe Spot wants to go and find the spoons and forks!" said Judy, with a laugh. "Well, we'll all go. Come on, Timmy."

All morning the two children and the dog tried to find where the biscuit tin could have been buried. They looked under hedges, they looked in ditches. They went across the fields and hunted everywhere to see if they could find a place where the earth had been newly dug.

But they couldn't. They just didn't see anywhere that was likely. Soon it was lunch-time and the two children were tired out.

"Let's go home," said Judy, with a sigh. "We can't find those spoons and forks, Timmy. Perhaps nobody will, and when the two burglars come out of prison they'll go and get them, and poor Mr Giles will never see them again. What a pity!"

Spot listened. He watched the children turn towards home but he didn't go with them. No, he had an idea of his own. He would go and hunt while they were having lunch. He had thought of a very good place.

As soon as the children were out of sight Spot ran off. He went to where a great pit had been dug out of the hillside for gravel and began to search there. It was a place that no one ever went to, for it was far from the lane and quite deserted.

Spot sniffed here and he sniffed there. His sharp little nose went under the prickly gorse bushes and into the blackberry brambles. He sniffed in this rabbit hole and in that, but for a long time it wasn't a bit of good.

"I shall have to give up," said Spot. "I'm feeling very hungry."

Just as he turned to go, a smell came to his nose. It was very faint but Spot knew what it was. Biscuits!

"Now there can't be any biscuits here, so it must be the hidden biscuit tin I can smell!" thought Spot excitedly. "I will find where this smell comes from."

He sniffed hard and then ran in the direction of the smell. It seemed to come from under a pile of stones. Spot ran to them. Yes, the smell certainly lay under the stones. Perhaps the burglars buried the tin of spoons and forks in the ground, and then piled stones on top to hide the newly turned earth.

The stones were big, but Spot managed to scratch them away. The biscuit smell was stronger than ever. He began to dig excitedly in the earth with his strong little paws.

Ah, what was that? His paws struck against something hard. Yes, it was a biscuit tin! Hurrah!

But Spot couldn't get the tin out of the earth, however much he tried. So off he ran to fetch Timmy and Judy. When he got home he tugged at Timmy's trousers, and the little boy guessed that he wanted him to follow where he led. So he and Judy set off after Spot.

When they came to where the biscuit tin was half dug up, how astonished they were! They opened the lid and there, neatly packed inside, were all Mr Giles's silver spoons and forks.

"Oh, you clever, clever little dog!" cried the children. "Come on, we'll take them to Mr Giles and get the reward."

Off they went, carrying the tin, and Mr Giles was most delighted to see them. He was very much astonished to hear how clever Spot had been.

"Here is the reward," he said. And what do you think it was? A whole ten pounds!

"Ooh!" cried the children in delight. "What a lovely present we can buy for Baby's birthday tomorrow. And something for clever little Spot too."

They ran to the shops and bought Baby a lovely cuddly bunny with big ears and a little white bobtail. Then they looked at Spot.

"We've got four pounds left," they told him. "What would you like for yourself?"

Spot chose a wonderful collar with tiny bells on, and a bar of chocolate. He marched home with his new collar outside and his chocolate inside. And when the other dogs met him and asked him why he had such a fine new collar, wasn't he proud to tell them!

The Adventurous Duck

Matthew had a bright new pound that his uncle had given him to spend. So he went to the toyshop on the seafront to buy something with it. He chose a very fine floating duck, and ran with it down to the sea.

It floated beautifully. It bobbed up and down on the waves and looked lovely. All the other boys and girls watched it and thought Matthew was very lucky.

But the duck was too adventurous. It floated out too far and Matthew couldn't get it back again. On it went and on and on, right out to sea. Matthew watched it sadly for it was a very beautiful duck.

Soon the duck was frightened. It couldn't see Matthew any more and the sea was very large and deep. Fishes swam about underneath it, and great seagulls sailed overhead.

"I wish I hadn't been so adventurous," said the duck sadly. "I wish I had kept close to Matthew. Now I shall be lost and never see him again."

Suddenly the duck gave a frightened quack and trembled all over its body. A big seagull was swooping nearer and nearer. At last it pounced on the little floating duck and picked it up in its yellow beak. Then away up in the air it flew, carrying the duck with it.

Higher and higher it went, and the other gulls came flying round to see what their friend held in his beak.

"Silly! Silly!" they cried. "It's nothing to eat. It's just a stupid toy."

The gull gave a screech and dropped the duck again. Down it fell, and down and down. Then, far below, it saw a boat full of people. A little girl was in it, and she suddenly saw the falling duck. She held out her hands and caught it just like a ball.

"Why, it's a dear little floating duck," she cried in astonishment. "Oh, I must take it out to tea with me this afternoon."

So when she was taken back to shore, and trotted off to go to tea with her auntie, she took the little duck with her. Her cousin was waiting for her at the gate and she waved to him.

"Come and look what I've got," she cried. "It's a dear little floating duck that fell out of a gull's beak!"

Now who do you suppose her cousin was? Why, it was Matthew! He stared at the duck in surprise for he could see that it was his.

"Why, that's the little duck I bought this morning with the pound your daddy gave me!" he said. "It floated right away and I saw a gull swoop down and pick it up."

"And it dropped it into my hands!" cried the little girl. "Oh, what an adventure it had, Matthew! Here it is, and I hope it will be a good duck now, and not go off by itself any more."

Matthew took it in delight. He thought he had lost it for ever. He was pleased, and the little girl was pleased, and as for the floating duck, it was so full of joy that it couldn't even quack!

Gillian and the Lamb

Once upon a time Gillian went down to the farm to fetch some eggs all by herself.

"I shall take my doll Betty with me in her pram," she said to her mother. "She has had a bad cold and the sunshine will do her good. I shan't be long, Mummy."

So Gillian tucked her doll up well, put her purse with the egg-money under the cover of the pram, and set out down the lane, feeling rather proud to think she was out by herself.

She went over the bridge and peeped at the brown stream underneath. She saw a great many white daisies in the grass, and some early buttercups. She heard a lark singing so high up in the sky that she couldn't see him at all.

"I hope you are enjoying this nice walk," she said to Betty, her doll, who was sitting up with her woolly hat on her curly hair.

Soon Gillian came to the
farm. There were so many hens
running about that she had to be
quite careful where she wheeled her doll's pram.

The hens said "Cluck, cluck!" to her in loud, cheerful voices
and she said "Cluck cluck!" back. It was easy to talk hen-
language.

She wheeled her pram up to the farm door. She knocked.
Nobody came. She knocked again, a bit harder this time. Still
nobody came.

"Oh dear," said Gillian. "That means no one is in – and I shall
have to go home without the eggs. What a pity!"

So she went off home again. She had just passed the field
where the big haystack stood when she saw something moving in
the hedge. She stopped to see what it was.

"Oh, it's a tiny baby lamb!" said Gillian, in surprise. "It's escaped from the field. Go back, lamb! If you don't, a car may come along and knock you down."

But the lamb wouldn't go back. It came limping over to Gillian, and then she saw that it had torn its leg on the barbed wire that ran along the hedges there. She kneeled down and looked at the leg.

"When I hurt my leg I have it bathed and some good stuff put on it," said Gillian. "Your mother sheep can't do that, but perhaps she will lick it better if you go back to her. Look – there she is, peeping through the hedge at you."

Sure enough, there was a big mother sheep putting her head through the hole in the hedge, baa-ing loudly. Gillian picked up the tiny lamb and carried it back to the hole – but it wouldn't go through it! It kept limping back to Gillian.

"Whatever shall I do with you, lamb?" she said. "I can't leave you here in the lane. And you won't go back to your mother. And there is no one at the farm this morning to look after you."

She stared at the lamb and the lamb stared back at Gillian. "Maa-aa-aa!" said the lamb, in a small, high voice, and it wriggled its tail like a hazel catkin on the hedge.

"I shall take you home to my own mother," said Gillian. "She is kind and will know what to do with you. She will make your leg better."

"Maa-aa-aa!" said the lamb.

"Come along then," said Gillian. "Walk close behind me, lamb." But the lamb wouldn't. It just stood there in the middle of the lane, maa-ing and wriggling its tail.

"Well, really, I don't know what to do with you!" said Gillian. And then an idea came into her head. Of course! She could wheel the lamb in her pram! It was quite small enough to go in.

So she picked up the tiny lamb and put it gently in the pram beside Betty, the doll. "I'm afraid you will be a bit squashed, Betty," said Gillian. "But I can't help it. Lie down, lamb. I'll cover you up nicely."

The lamb was surprised to find himself in a pram. He lay quite still. Gillian covered him up. She tucked him in well in case he wriggled loose. "Maa-aa-aa!" said the lamb, and he sniffed at Betty, the doll.

Gillian wheeled the pram up the lane. She met Mr Logs, the woodman. "Good morning," he said. "And how's your doll today?"

"She's a bit squashed because she's sharing the pram with a lamb," said Gillian. Mr Logs bent to see – and when he saw the little lamb looking at him, how he laughed.

"That's a funny sight!" he said. "Well, well, well!"

Then Gillian met Mrs Thimble, who did sewing for lots of people. "Good morning, Gillian," she said. "And how's your doll today?"

"She's a bit squashed because she's sharing the pram with a lamb," said Gillian. Mrs Thimble bent down to see, and how she laughed when the little lamb said "Maa-aa-aa!" to her.

"No, I'm not your maa-aa-aa," she said. "I can hear your ma baa-ing for you in the field."

"Oh, there's Mummy," said Gillian. "I must go and show her my lamb. Goodbye."

She wheeled the pram in at the gate of Old Thatch. Her mother was weeding a flowerbed nearby. She called her.

"Mummy. Here's a lamb with a hurt leg. It wouldn't go back into its field, and there's no one at the farm so I've brought it home for you to mend."

Her mother stood up in astonishment and looked for the lamb. She didn't think of looking into the pram.

"Where is the lamb?" she said.

"Maa–aa–aa!" said the lamb, waving one of its feet over the pram cover. How Gillian's mother laughed! She laughed and she laughed to see the lamb lying in the pram with Betty, the doll.

"Whatever will you do next, Gillian?" she said. She took the lamb out of the pram and looked at its leg.

"Go and get me a basin of water," she said. So Gillian ran off. Very soon the lamb's leg was washed and some good stuff put on it. It wasn't very badly hurt. It didn't even need a bandage, though Gillian wanted to put one on.

Just then the farmer's wife came by the gate, home from shopping, and she looked in. How surprised she was to see the lamb in the garden!

Gillian told her all about it, and the farmer's wife laughed when she heard about the lamb being wheeled in the pram.

"Thank you for being kind enough to look after it for me," she said to Gillian. "I'll carry it back to the field now, and mend the fence."

So she did – but always after that, when Gillian went down the lane, the little lamb watched for her and maa-ed to her. It puts its tiny head through the hedge and you may be sure that Gillian always stops to rub its little black nose!

Funny-Face

The children had been to a party and they had brought a funny balloon back with them. It had a smiling face painted on it, and feathers gummed to the top for hair. It was really very funny.

Jane hung it from the centre light, twisting the string round it so that the balloon swung to and fro below. "Funny-Face," she said. "I wonder what the toys will think of you, grinning away like that."

They went to bed and left Funny-Face swinging gently to and fro. The toys came out and looked at it.

"Who are you?" said the clown. Funny-Face didn't say a word. It just swung gently to and fro, smiling and smiling. The feathers on the top quivered as if they were laughing too.

"It's rude to grin like that and never say a word," said the bear. "What is your proper name? We heard the children calling you Funny-Face."

Funny-Face just smiled and said nothing. The clown got very angry.

"Who do you think you are, swinging there above our heads and laughing at us?" he said. "Come down and tell us your name."

To his great surprise Funny-Face swung faster, and then the string slipped from the light and the balloon floated gently down to the toys. The wind had blown in at the window that very minute and loosened the string.

The toys were scared when they saw Funny-Face so near to them. They ran away. Funny-Face smiled and smiled.

The clown soon felt bold when he saw that Funny-Face didn't chase the toys. He came out from his corner.

"Ho! So you've come down to join us. Well, perhaps you will tell us your name now?"

Funny-Face rolled about a little and didn't say one word. The clown marched right up to it and glared. He was rather bossy.

"I smack people who don't answer me," he said, and he gave the balloon a big smack. It bounced away and then rolled back again, still smiling.

"I don't like your smile," said the bold clown. "Stop smiling! And answer me when I speak to you!"

Funny-Face didn't answer. It rolled a little way away from the clown in the wind that came under the door. The clown went after it.

"I shall smack you with both my hands and kick you with both my feet if you aren't polite enough to say who you are!" he said. And will you believe it, he did just as he said – and, of course, Funny-Face bobbed right away to the other side of the room. It knocked over a little toy soldier as it went and the soldier squealed.

"Use your bayonet, soldier," shouted the clown. "He's getting fierce. How dare he knock you over!"

So the soldier held his bayonet, and as the balloon bobbed near him again he pointed it at Funny-Face and shouted, "Any nearer and I will fight you!"

The balloon couldn't help going nearer because the wind under the door blew it again. It bobbed smiling right on to the soldier's sharp bayonet.

What a noise! The toys all fell over and then sat up again in surprise, looking for Funny-Face.

"He's gone," said the clown.

"But he's left his feathers behind," said the soldier.

"And his string," said the bear. "Where's he gone? I can't see him anywhere. Did we frighten him away?"

"He must have flown out of the window," said the clown. "But what was that terrible bang?"

Nobody knew. They were all very scared and they crept into the toy-cupboard and were soon fast asleep.

Jane heard the bang and got out of bed. She padded into the playroom and saw the burst balloon – just a bit of rubber and string and feathers lying on the floor.

"Oh dear! Funny-Face has popped," she said. "Why did you, Funny-Face? I do wish I knew."

Well, I'm afraid she'll never know – unless she reads this story!

The Goblin in the Train

All the toys were most excited. Tomorrow the clockwork train was going to take them to a pixie party, and what fun that would be. But, oh dear, wasn't it a shame, when Andrew was playing with the train that day, he overwound it and broke the spring. Then it wouldn't go, and all the toys crowded round it that night, wondering what they would do the next night when they wanted to go to the party.

"I'm very sorry," said the clockwork train. "But I simply can't move a wheel, you know. My spring is quite broken. You won't be able to go to the pixie party, because I can't take you. It's all Andrew's fault."

"Well, he must have broken your spring by accident," said the rag-doll. "He's very careful with us, generally. But it is dreadfully disappointing."

"Couldn't we send a message to the little goblin who lives under the holly bush?" said the teddy bear. "He is very clever at mending things, and he might be able to mend the broken spring."

"Good idea!" cried the toys, and they at once sent a message to the goblin. He came in five minutes, and shook his head when he saw the broken spring.

"This will take me a long time to mend," he said. "I doubt if I'll get it done by cock-crow."

"Please, please try!" cried the toys. So he set to work. He had all sorts of strange tools, not a bit like ours, and he worked away as hard as ever he could. And suddenly, just as he had almost finished, a cock crowed! That meant that all toys and fairy folk must scuttle away to their own places again, but the goblin couldn't bear to leave his job unfinished.

"I'll just pop into the cab of the train," he called to the toys. "I'll make myself look like a little driver, and as Andrew knows the spring is broken, perhaps he won't look at the train today or notice me. Then I can quickly finish my work tonight and you'll be able to go to the party."

The toys raced off to their cupboard, thinking how very kind the goblin was. He hopped into the cab, sat down there, and kept quite still, just as if he were the driver.

Andrew didn't once look at his engine that day and the toys were so glad. When night came again the goblin set to work and very soon he had finished mending the spring. He wound up the engine, and hey presto, its wheels went round and it raced madly round the room.

"Good! Good!" cried the toys. "Now we can go to the party. Hurrah! What can we do to return your kindness, goblin?"

"Well," said the goblin, turning rather red, "there is one thing I'd like. You know, I'm rather an ugly little chap, and I've never been asked to a pixie party in my life. I suppose you wouldn't take me with you? If you would I'd drive the train, and see that nothing went wrong with it."

"Of course, of course!" shouted the toys in glee. "You shall come with us, goblin, and we'll tell the pixies how nice you are."

Then they all got into the train, the goblin wound it up again, and they went to the party. What a glorious time they had, and what a hero the goblin was when the toys had finished telling everyone how he had mended the broken train.

He drove them all safely back home again and then, guess what? He was so happy and so tired that he fell fast asleep sitting in the cab!

And in the morning Andrew found him there and was so surprised.

"Look, Mummy, look!" he shouted. "The train has suddenly got a driver, and gosh, the spring is mended too! Isn't that a strange thing, and isn't he a nice little driver? Wherever could he have come from?"

But his mother couldn't think how he could have got there.

"He must have been there all the time and you didn't notice him before," she said.

"No, Mummy, really," said Andrew. "I've often wished my clockwork train had a driver, and I know I should have noticed him if he had been here before. Oh, I do hope he stays. He looks so nice and real."

The goblin was so happy to find that Andrew liked him and was pleased with him. But he was happier still that night when all the toys crowded round him and begged him to stay and be one of them.

"We like you very much," they said. "Don't go back to your holly bush, but stay here and be the driver of Andrew's train. We'll have such fun together every night."

The goblin wanted nothing better than to stay where he was, for he had often been very lonely under his holly bush.

"I'd love to stay," he said. "Come on, I'll take you for a fine ride, round and round the room." The toys almost woke Andrew up with their shouts of delight.

Andrew is very proud of his train driver. He shows him to everyone, and I do hope you'll see him for yourself some day. Then perhaps you can tell Andrew the story of how he got there.

The Lovely Present

The Little Princess Peronel had been ill. The king and queen were glad when she began to get better, and they hoped very much she would soon be happy and bright again. It was dreadful to see her looking so sad.

In the middle of November the princess had her birthday, and the king meant to make it a very grand affair.

Perhaps the princess would cheer up when she saw all her presents arriving, he thought, and he decided to send out a notice to say that everyone must try to think of something really good this year.

As soon as the people knew that the king hoped for plenty of amusing presents for Peronel, they set to work to make them, for they all loved the little girl. One carved a big wooden bear that could open its mouth and growl. One made a whistle that could sing like a bird, from an elder twig. There were all sorts of lovely presents!

There was one small boy who badly wanted to give the princess something, but he couldn't think what. He had no money. He couldn't carve a toy. He couldn't even make a whistle. He really didn't know *what* to do.

And then one day he did a very strange thing. It was a windy morning and the last leaves were blowing down from the trees. The little boy went out with a small sack. He stood under the trees, and every time the wind blew down a gust of dry leaves he tried to catch one. All that day he worked and all the next. In fact, he worked for nine days without stopping, and by that time his sack was quite full.

Then, on the birthday morning, he set out to the palace with the sack of leaves on his back. Everyone wondered what he had. Hundreds of other people were on the way, too, all with toys and presents. But alas for the king's hopes. Not one of the presents made the sad little princess even smile.

Towards the last of all came the small boy with his sack. "What have you got there?" asked the king, in surprise.

"A year of happy days for the little princess!" said the boy. He opened his sack and emptied all the dry, rustling leaves over the surprised princess. Everyone stared in astonishment.

"Don't you know that for every leaf you catch in the autumn, before it touches the ground, you will have a happy day next year?" said the little boy to the princess. "Well, I have caught three hundred and sixty-five for you, so that's a whole year. They're for you, because I'd like you to be happy and well again – so here they all are! And, as this is the first day of your new birthday year, you must smile and be happy!"

And she did, because she was so pleased.

Just Big Enough for Him!

"I think I'll clean out my doll's-house this morning," said Helen to her mother. "I'll take it down to the shed, Mummy."

Soon Helen was very busy indeed. She carried her doll's-house down to the shed and put it on the floor there. She opened the front of the house and set to work. First she took all the furniture out. Then she washed the floors and the walls and shook the little carpets.

Then she cleaned all the furniture and put it back again. She made the two small beds and wiped round the tiny bath.

"There!" she said. "Now it all looks very nice. I think I'll leave it down here till I've washed the curtains."

She took the tiny curtains
back to wash, and left the
spick-and-span doll's-house in the
shed. But it was lunch-time when she
got in, and she hadn't time to wash the
curtains. She popped them into the toy-
cupboard and forgot all about them.

She didn't remember them till the next week. Then she
washed them carefully, ironed them with her toy iron, and took
them to the shed.

The door was open a little. She went inside and saw Tibby
the cat sitting there, looking very solemn indeed.

"Why, Tibby – so it's here you come to when we miss you!"
said Helen, surprised.

"Miaow!" said Tibby. He pressed his face close against one of
the doll's-house windows, exactly as if he were looking inside.
Then he scraped at the front door which was half open.

"What are you doing?" said Helen, in surprise. "Tibby, surely you don't think you're small enough to get into my doll's-house! Take your paw out of the front."

"Miaow!" said Tibby, and put his paw in at the door as far as it would go. Then he put his face down to the doorway and sniffed hard.

"Really! Anyone would think you wanted to live here," said Helen, pushing him away. "Cats don't live in doll's-houses!"

But Tibby wouldn't go away. He pressed his face against a window again. Helen pushed him away once more and peeped in herself. What she saw there gave her a very big surprise.

Someone was in one of the little beds! Someone was curled up there, fast asleep, the tiny blanket half over him. Who could it be?

Helen felt very excited. Her heart began to beat fast. Who had found her doll's-house and gone to sleep in one of the beds? Taking Tibby in her arms, she put him outside the shed door and shut it. No wonder he was so interested in the doll's-house.

She opened the front of the house very carefully and looked into the bedroom. On one of the beds lay a small, furry creature, so fast asleep that he didn't even wake when Helen touched him.

"It must be a mouse – or a kind of a mouse," said Helen, delighted. "A very small, round one – and dear me, look at his long, fluffy tail all curled round him.
Oh, he's sweet! He's a pet! Oh,
what will Mummy say?"

She decided to shut the front of the doll's-house and carry it up to her own house to show her mother. Tibby was outside, waiting for her.

Mother could hardly believe her eyes when she saw the tiny animal on the bed. "Why – it's a dormouse!" she said. "What a poppet!"

"Mummy, why doesn't he wake up? Why did he choose my doll's-house bed to sleep in?" asked Helen.

"Well, it's autumn now and the cold weather has begun," said Mother. "Lots of tiny creatures sleep the whole winter through – and the dormouse is one of them. Usually they choose a hole somewhere – or perhaps the bottom of a flowerpot in a shed – but this one wandered into the shed and found your doll's-house door open and went inside. He curled up on the bed, the little dear."

"Will he sleep there all the winter?" asked Helen, delighted.

"Yes, if we keep him in a fairly cold place," said her mother. "You'll have to take your doll's-house back to the shed – it's cold there in the winter. He'll sleep well, then, and won't wake till the warm springtime!"

Helen was so happy. To think of a dormouse choosing to sleep the winter away in a tiny doll's bed in her doll's-house! "I'm lucky," she said, "very, very lucky. I don't believe anyone else in the world has a doll's-house with a dormouse sleeping in it."

So there he is curled up under the blanket that Helen put over him, his tiny nose buried in his paws, fast asleep. Won't she be sorry when he wakes up in the springtime and runs off to play in the woods he loves?

The Old Boot

There was once an old boot. It lay in a ditch, burst open at the toes, worn down at the heel and with its laces missing. Once it had been a very grand boot – so grand that it had been worn by a prince. Think of that! It had been proud then, with a servant to polish it up every day and to make it shine brilliantly. Its brother boot lived with it, and they talked together all day long, very happily.

Then the prince bought some new boots and gave his old ones to his servant. The man was proud to have such grand boots and wore them every Sunday – but when they wanted mending he couldn't be bothered with them. He told his wife to give them away at the door next time a pedlar came round with some plants. So the boots were given to a ragged old pedlar and he gave the servant's wife a fine fern for them.

They did not fit the pedlar very well, especially one of them, for his right foot was much bigger than his left. They were never cleaned now, and never mended. They grew old and wrinkled, and one of them burst at the toes. The pedlar grumbled bitterly at the boots, and one day, when he found an old shoe by the roadside, he flung off one of the boots, put on the shoe instead, and threw the old boot into the ditch. Then, limping, he went off down the road, wearing one boot and one shoe.

Then the old boot in the ditch was lonely, for it no longer had its brother boot to talk with. Spiders ran over it. A beetle went inside it. The rain soaked it through and through, and some grass seeds took root inside and grew there. The boot was sad and ashamed to think what it had come to. No one cared about it now, lost and forgotten in a wayside ditch.

Then one day in spring a red-breasted robin flew down to the ditch and turned over some dead leaves there. He saw the old boot and perched on the side, peering this way and that. Then he uttered a little trill and called his wife to him.

"Look! What a wonderful place for a nest. You know how we robins love to build in something that has belonged to man, our friend. Well, here is a splendid boot, just right for a nest. What a piece of luck!"

Then, to the great delight of the old boot, the robins built their nest there. How carefully they built it of grass-roots, fibres, moss and leaves. The boot marvelled at the way they used their beaks to weave such a cosy home. It liked to feel their tiny feet perching here and there, and loved to listen to their creamy voices when they sang.

Four speckled eggs were laid in the old boot. How proud it was, and how much prouder when the eggs hatched out into tiny birds, which were soon covered with softest down and feathers. It listened contentedly to their chatter, and was excited when they first tried their tiny wings.

"Thank you, old boot," sang the robins, when their youngsters had all flown. "You kept our family safe!"

The boot was lonely when the robins were gone – but an adventure was still to come to it. For one day two children found it, with the old robins' nest still inside.

"A find, a find!" they cried. "Let's take it to school, and put it in the museum there. Everyone will love to see it."

They did, and now the old boot has the place of honour in the school museum and is as happy as can be.